EXPRESS NEWSPAPERS plc, Ludgate House,
245 Blackfriars Road,
London SE1 9UX.

Produced by Brainwaves Limited
5 Highwood Ridge, Hatch Warren, Basingstoke,
Hampshire RG22 4UU.

ISBN 0–85079–247–9

RUPERT

and the
Popweed

It's holiday time once again! This year
Mr and Mrs Bear have decided to go back to
Rocky Bay. 'We had such wonderful fun last
time we were here,' says Mrs Bear.

So that Rupert will have someone to play
with, his parents have asked Bill Badger to
come along too. 'I'm glad you asked me!'
says Bill, as they all walk down to the sea,
'I love Rocky Bay!' 'I can't wait to build
some sandcastles on the beach!' grins
Rupert, clutching his new bucket and spade.

As soon as they arrive at the beach the two pals rush over to see Cap'n Binnacle, an old seafarer they met the last time they were in Rocky Bay. 'Hello Cap'n!' shouts Rupert. 'Remember us?' 'Of course!' replies the old man. 'You're the pair from Nutwood!'

He tells Rupert and Bill that there have been very rough, stormy seas lately, and that some interesting things have been washed up. 'Come and have a look,' he says. 'I'll show you what I've found!'

'Last week we had the worst storm I've ever
seen!' says Cap'n Binnacle, as they walk up
to his little shack. 'And you'll never
believe what I picked up on the beach the
next day!'

On a table in the shack is spread out a
huge collection of big, beautiful shells
that Cap'n Binnacle has found on the beach.
'Gosh!' exclaims Rupert, 'They're wonderful!'
'Yes!' agrees Bill, 'I'd love to find some
like that myself!'

Going back down to the beach where Rupert's
Mother and Father have set up their deck
chairs, Rupert and Bill decide that they
will try and find some shells for
themselves. 'What fun!' says Bill.

When Rupert tells his parents what they're
going to do, his father suggests that they
split up and have a competition, 'Why don't
you see who can get the best collection?' he
says. 'But don't go too far!' Rupert's
Mother calls after the pals.

While Bill sets off to explore one end of the beach, Rupert clambers onto a rock to see what he can find. 'There's nothing here at all,' he says to himself as he looks around. 'Perhaps the tide is too high. I'll have to try again later.'

Just then he spots a long, thin strand of seaweed which looks like a piece of green string. Pulling it in, he finds that it's covered in large black bobbles. 'I wonder what sort of weed this is?' thinks Rupert.

Rupert dashes back to show his parents what he has found. 'I've never seen anything like this before!' he says excitedly, holding up the seaweed.

'When I was your age,' says Mrs Bear, 'we used to find seaweed with lots of tiny bobbles on it – we used to pop them, didn't we Father?' 'That's right,' says Rupert's Daddy, 'but they were never as large as this. Why don't you take it up to show Cap'n Binnacle? Perhaps he'll know what it is.'

'Have you had any luck yet?' asks the Cap'n
when Rupert finds him. 'Not really,' replies
Rupert. 'All I've found is this seaweed – my
Mummy says it's like the sort she used to
pop when she was my age, only much bigger.'

Cap'n Binnacle looks at the seaweed. 'We
called it popweed when we were lads,' he
says. 'Why don't you squeeze it and see if
it'll pop too?' Rupert presses hard on one
of the black bobbles, and it pops with a
tremendous noise!

'Good gracious me!' exclaims Cap'n Binnacle, 'I've not heard anything like that since last Guy Fawkes Night!' 'It was rather loud,' agrees Rupert.

As Cap'n Binnacle is examining the weed, Rupert looks out to sea. 'Cap'n!' he calls, 'Look what's happening out there!' Turning round, the old Cap'n sees that all kinds of fish are leaping madly out of the water. 'Anyone would think a shark had come into the bay!' he gasps.

Bless my buttons!' says Cap'n Binnacle,
raising his eyebrows. 'I've never seen
anything like that in all my born days!'
'What made it happen?' asks Rupert.

Cap'n Binnacle says that he has no idea what
might be going on. 'But if it *is* a shark,'
he says gravely, 'I'd better get over to
the coastguard quickly, and warn them to
stop people swimming hereabouts!' Leaving
Rupert staring at the sea, which has by now
calmed down, the Cap'n rushes off.

Rupert decides to go off and explore some more of the shoreline, 'I was probably looking in the wrong place for shells,' he thinks to himself. 'I'll go around the bay and have a look at the next inlet!'

Taking care not to slip as he climbs over the rocks, Rupert clambers into the next little bay. On the other side he spots a large, flat rock sticking out into the sea. 'That looks like a good place to start my search,' he says.

On his way over to the rock, Rupert looks for any shells that might have been washed up, but he's out of luck. 'I'm *never* going to win the competition with Bill at this rate!' he sighs.

As soon as he's on the rock, Rupert sees some more of the giant seaweed. 'There's no one around to mind the noise,' he thinks to himself, 'so I'll pop another popweed bobble, just for fun!' Pressing as hard as he can, Rupert bursts the big, black bobble.

To Rupert's surprise, the seaweed makes a
noise that's even louder than the first time
he popped a bobble, 'More of a bang than a
pop!' thinks Rupert, as the echoes bounce
off the cliffs.

He's just about to try popping another
one when, to his astonishment, the sea in
front of him shoots up in a pillar of water,
with fish flapping wildly in the air.
'Crikey!' gasps Rupert, as he falls over
backwards. 'Whatever have I done!'

Sitting up and brushing off the salty water that has fallen on him, Rupert hears a splashing noise. 'Who's there?' he demands, turning round sharply.

There behind him on the rock, Rupert is amazed to see a little merboy. 'So it was *you* that sounded the alarm!' exclaims the merboy angrily. 'Don't you realise that setting off false alarms is a crime? And *where* did you get the popweed? Only King Neptune's subjects are allowed to use it!'

'I'm sorry if I've done anything wrong,' apologises Rupert. 'I had no idea I was sounding any kind of alarm!' 'Well you were,' replies the merboy, 'and we've got to sort things out!'

'How are we going to do that?' asks Rupert. 'Wait a second,' says the merboy, diving back into the water. Moments later Rupert nearly joins him when a huge sea serpent rises up out of the waves. 'Help!' shouts Rupert. 'A monster!'

Reappearing on the rock, the merboy tells
Rupert not to worry. 'He's just come to take
you to the court of King Neptune, that's
all!' 'But I don't want to go to court,'
cries Rupert, 'I want to go home!'

'You haven't got much choice,' points out
the merboy, looking at the sea. 'The tide's
come in and you can't get back to the beach
without us!' Realising that the merboy is
right, Rupert agrees to get on the sea
serpent's back.

As he looks at the smooth, scaly back of the sea serpent, Rupert becomes worried. 'He's so slippery, I'm sure I'll fall off!' he says to the merboy. 'Don't be frightened!' he replies. 'I promise you, it's impossible to slip off!'

Rupert climbs gingerly onto the sea serpent's back, and hangs on as tight as he can. Swimming beside him, the merboy smiles broadly, 'I told you it would be all right,' he grins, as they speed through the water.

In quite a short time Rupert is amazed to
see a small dot appear on the horizon.
'Neptune's Island!' says the merboy, 'You'll
have to wait here for a bit.'

Getting off the sea serpent's back, Rupert
stands on a rock. 'What happens now?' he asks
the merboy. 'I've got to go and see the
Judge,' says the merboy, 'to tell him that
I've found the cause of the popweed alarms –
I'll be back very soon!' Telling Rupert to
wait, the merboy dives beneath the waves.

Watching the sea serpent swim away, Rupert
realises that he is now all alone on the
island. 'Well I *suppose* I'm alone,' he says
to himself. 'But I'd better have a good look
round, just to make sure!'

As he begins to climb up the nearby cliff,
Rupert can't make out why so much fuss is
being made about some silly old seaweed that
goes *bang!* instead of *pop!* 'It doesn't make
sense,' he thinks to himself, 'and it
certainly isn't *my* fault!'

Nearing the top of the cliff, Rupert suddenly stops. 'I'm sure I heard voices,' he murmurs. 'Yes, there they are again! There's someone else here after all!'

Thinking that whoever is on the island may be able to help him get back to Rocky Bay, Rupert pokes his head over the top of the cliff to see who the voices belong to. 'It's too far,' he says as he peers down. 'I can't see properly from up here, but it looks like a group of sailors!'

It's not until it's too late to turn back
that Rupert realises he's made a mistake.
'They're pirates!' he thinks, as the men
turn to see who's coming down the cliff.
'And they don't look pleased to see me!'

'Avast there!' shouts a bearded man in a
tricorn hat. 'What be ye doin' here? *Spyin'*
on us young fellow me lad, that's what ye be
doin', ain't it?' 'No!' exclaims Rupert.
'You don't understand – I'm just looking for
someone to help me to get off this island!'

'Well that's as may be!' sneers the priate captain. 'But this is supposed to be our *secret* hide-out. You'll have to stay here awhile till we've finished our business!' So saying, the pirate orders one of his men to take Rupert away.

As Rupert is marched into a cave he notices a big pile of boxes, 'It looks like stolen treasure,' thinks Rupert, 'I'm in worse trouble than ever!' 'Now don't move until we fetch you!' orders the sailor gruffly.

Noticing that light is coming into the cave from behind him, Rupert climbs up and finds a hole in the rocks. 'Maybe I can escape,' he says. 'I'm sure being back with the merboy would be better than staying a prisoner of these dreadful pirates!'

As he is about to look out of the hole he has discovered, Rupert is surprised to hear a voice behind him. 'Don't leave without me!' it pleads. Rupert looks round to find a boy hiding in the shadows.

'Who are you?' asks Rupert, delighted to find a friend in this awful place. 'My name is Jon,' replies the boy. 'I live near Rocky Bay, and rowed out to this island to explore it – I was captured by the pirates, just like you!'

'Here,' he says, after finishing his story, 'have a bite to eat, you must be hungry – you can share the food they've given me.' 'Thanks,' says Rupert, 'but what are we going to do? We can't stay here!'

'I overheard them talking,' says Jon.
'They're only waiting for their ship to come
back from another raid, so we must escape
from here as soon as possible!' 'You're
right!' agrees Rupert. 'I don't want to
spend the rest of my life at sea!'

Finishing their food, Rupert and Jon climb
out of the hole at the back of the cave and
clamber along the rocks until they reach the
water's edge. 'So far, so good,' says
Rupert. 'But what do we do now?'

'If I'm not mistaken,' says Jon, 'we're quite near where I tied up my boat when I landed here! Let's see if I'm right . . .'

Picking their way over the rocks, the pals are led into a small inlet. There, rocking gently in the water, is a small rowing boat. 'They haven't found it!' cries Jon, smiling. Then all of a sudden his face falls. 'What's the matter?' asks Rupert. 'The oars must have fallen out – now we'll *never* get away!' moans Jon.

'I've an idea that might just get us out of this!' smiles Rupert. 'Come on, let's go to that rock over there.' 'Be careful,' says Jon, 'they might spot us!' Rupert tells him not to worry, and reaching into his trouser pocket, he takes out some of the giant popweed bobbles that he'd kept.

'What are you going to do with those?' queries Jon. 'How is seaweed going to help us?' Telling him to wait and see, Rupert squeezes hard on one of the bobbles.

There is another massive explosion, the loudest so far, and like before, as its echoes die away, the sea begins to boil with leaping fish. 'How *did* you do that?' says an amazed Jon, his ears still ringing from the popweed boom.

'It's a little trick I know!' grins Rupert. 'Now we'll just have to hope that it works like it did the last time.' 'You mean you've done this before?' gasps Jon. 'You must be some sort of magician!'

Before Rupert has time to answer, the sea serpent appears, snaking out of the water like a scaly, green pole. 'You *are* a magician!' shouts Jon, running for safety behind a rock. 'I think I preferred being a prisoner!'

'It's quite all right!' cries Rupert. 'He's very friendly, come and see!' Turning to the sea serpent, Rupert explains that after the merboy left he was captured by pirates. 'And now we need your help.' he says.

The noise of the popweed explosion was so loud that the pirates have heard it. Led by their captain, they come running round the cove. 'Them boys has esca . . .!' yells the leader, skidding to a halt on the slippery rocks. 'Shiver me timbers! But what's *that!*' he says, on seeing the sea serpent.

One roar from the scaly monster is enough to make the pirates turn on their heels and run. 'That's one problem dealt with,' smiles Rupert. 'Now there's just King Neptune . . .'

'What *about* King Neptune?' asks Jon. 'It's against the law in his underwater kingdom to burst the popweed, except in an emergency,' explains Rupert, 'and *I'm* not supposed to have any in the first place!'

At that moment, the merboy wooshes up out of the sea and onto the rock where the pals are standing. 'The Judge is ready to see you now,' he says, 'and he doesn't like to be kept waiting!' Rupert tells the merboy about Jon, and he agrees to take him with them.

Calling to the sea serpent, the little
merboy tells him that there is now an extra
person to carry. 'He says he can't take two
passengers,' says the merboy. 'But he'll
come back for the boy later.'

'But I've a boat,' cries Jon, 'though there
aren't any oars – couldn't he tow us?'
'Could the serpent do that?' Rupert asks the
merboy. Thinking for a moment, the merboy
replies, 'I *suppose* he can, though I don't
think he's done anything like it before!'

While Jon gets the boat ready, the merboy apologises to Rupert about the pirates. 'I had no idea there was anyone here,' he says. 'This island has always been deserted. King Neptune doesn't like pirates, but I don't expect *they'll* be back here in a hurry!'

'This should be fun!' grins Rupert, as the pals settle down in the little boat. Jon throws the rope to the sea serpent, who catches it in his mouth, and the merboy shouts 'Off we go!'

Joining Rupert and Jon in the boat, the merboy grins, 'I'm going to ride with you two,' he says. 'I think I've swum far enough for one day!'

Leaving the island behind them, the odd-looking convoy sets out across the water. 'It's not far now,' says the merboy, in reply to Rupert's question as to when they'll get there. 'In fact that's the cave entrance now!' he says, diving back into the water and swimming alongside the boat.

Dropping the rope, the sea serpent sinks out of view without a word, and the merboy pushes the boat into the cave. 'Now, you must come with me,' he says to Rupert. 'There's no time to waste!'

'But what about me?' asks Jon. 'What am I supposed to do?' 'You must wait here,' replies the merboy. 'You're not allowed into the court!' Telling Jon that he'll bring Rupert back as soon as he can, the merboy leads the little bear deep into the cave.

The merboy takes Rupert into the heart of the island. 'I wonder what's at the end of this tunnel?' thinks Rupert as he stumbles along the narrow, winding path.

As the path straightens out, he can see a strange glow, and seconds later they enter a large cavern. At one end sits a bespectacled octopus wearing a wig. 'Oh no!' says Rupert. 'He looks very serious!' 'I'm ready to hear the case of the stolen popweed,' declares the Judge. 'Bring forward the defendant!'

Rupert timidly steps forward. 'I found the popweed on the beach at Rocky Bay, your honour,' he says in a small voice. 'I didn't steal it, honestly!' 'Hmmmph!' replies the Judge, picking up a book and peering at it.

Looking up sternly, the Judge squints over his glasses. 'I see there was a force 10 storm around Rocky Bay last week,' he says, 'and that must have washed the popweed up onto the beach! There's no case to answer – you're free to go, little bear!'

'Phew!' sighs Rupert, on hearing the Judge's decision. 'Can I go home now?' he asks the merboy, as they go back down the passage to where they have left Jon.

'Of course!' grins the merboy. 'But as I didn't think the sea serpent would be very happy to tow your boat again, I've asked someone else to do the job instead!' Leaping out of the water, Rupert and Jon spot the biggest fish either of them has ever seen coming towards them!

Saying goodbye to the merboy, and promising
never to burst any more popweed, Rupert
throws the tow rope out to the big fish.
'Here you are!' he cries. Grabbing it in its
mouth, the fish turns with a flick of its
tail and speeds off towards Rocky Bay.

'This is better than a speed-boat!' laughs
Rupert as they skip across the waves. 'Well
it's certainly better than rowing!' grins
Jon. 'And look – there's Rocky Bay just
behind that headland!'

From the look-out in his shack, old Cap'n
Binnacle spots Rupert and Jon as they land
on the beach. 'Bless my boots!' he exclaims.
'There's Rupert – and he's got young Jon
with him! I wonder how they met up?'

As Cap'n Binnacle greets the pals, Rupert's
parents arrive with Bill. 'We've been
looking for you *everywhere!*' he cries.
'What have you been up to?' asks Rupert's
Mummy. 'I think I need a bite to eat before
I can even begin to tell you!' says Rupert.

Mrs Bear spreads out a tablecloth on the beach and they all sit down to have some tea. 'Well,' says Cap'n Binnacle, 'let's hear your story then!'

When he has finished telling the amazing tale of all the adventures he has had because of the popweed, and Jon has told them about how he was captured by pirates, Rupert sits back. 'And to think this all began because Bill and I were searching for shells!' he says.